# PUSHKI´S
## FIRST TRAIN ADVENTURE

Prashansa Meyn

Illustrations

By

**Revathi Balaji**

INDIA · SINGAPORE · MALAYSIA

**Notion Press**

Old No. 38, New No. 6
McNichols Road, Chetpet
Chennai - 600 031

First Published by Notion Press 2019
Copyright © Prashansa Meyn 2019
All Rights Reserved.

ISBN 978-1-68466-998-1

For,

Tony

# Contents

# Some help with the Indian words

| Word | Language | Meaning |
| --- | --- | --- |
| *Ammamma* | Telugu | Maternal grandmother |
| *Tatagaru* | Telugu | Maternal grandfather |
| *Madras* | English | Former name of the South-Indian city of Chennai, Tamil Nadu |
| *Samosa* | Hindi | Savory fried snack popular across India, made usually with a potato filling |
| *Idly* | Tamil | South Indian dish, steamed rice cakes |
| *Dosa* | Tamil | South Indian dish, crispy crepe-like savory dish made with fermented rice and lentil dough |
| *Vada* | Tamil, Hindi | Savory fried snack from India, made like fritters; has a doughnut-like shape |
| *Pongal* | Tamil | Spicy rice dish made with rice, lentils, pepper, cashew nuts and curry leaves |
| *Poha* | Marathi, Hindi | Breakfast dish from western India (mainly Maharashtra) using flattened rice, potato, groundnuts and spices |
| *Poori* | Hindi | Popular Indian breakfast. It is a type of unleavened deep-fried bread, eaten usually with a savory potato side-dish or a sweet-dish called Halwa. |
| *Aloo* | Hindi | Potato |
| *Coolie* | Hindi | Unskilled laborer |

# Chapter 1

# **Holidays**

Pushki was very excited for it was the holiday season again. Twice every year, she visited her grandparents in Madhya Pradesh, Central India. Pushki and her mother would visit her maternal grandparents, once during the summer vacation and next in the winter vacation. It was going to be winter again and Pushki could not wait for the holidays to begin. As Pushki's little sister Rinki was born in the summer earlier that year, they did not visit her *ammamma* and *tatagaru* in the summer and since it was almost a year from her previous visit, Pushki was most excited about the upcoming holiday.

The year was 1993 and Pushki was seven years old. She was in class one and had plans of becoming the class leader in class two. She liked bossing over the boys in her class and she felt having the class leader badge would help her immensely in doing just that. With that thought, Pushki finished her last exam of the season, hugged her best friend Jaya goodbye and yelled, *"Happy holidays, Merry Christmas and a very happy new year in advance!"* to every person in her school portico and rushed out to meet her father, who was waiting for her at the school gate.

*"DADDY! Has mummy finished packing? Is Rinki still asleep? Can I sit at the window seat? Oh wait, can I climb up and sleep on the top berth?"*

*"Ha! Ha! calm down sweetheart,"* Pushki's daddy replied. He continued, *"Of course mummy has finished packing and yes, your sister is only 8 months old now, so she sleeps a lot. But, when she grows up and becomes as big as you, you can talk and play with her…"*

*"But daddy, when she is as big as me, won't I be bigger?,"* quipped Pushki. *"Oh no! Just imagine, when she is going to be in primary school, I will be in middle school and then when she is in middle school, I will be in high school and when she comes to high school, I will be in college and when she comes to college......"*

*"Now, now, Pushki, didn't you want the window seat?,"* asked daddy desperate to divert Pushki's attention. *"Feels like you were born just now, Pushki, and see, you are already making college plans,"* he thought to himself with a smile.

*"Oh yes! I want the window seat and I want Frooti, cashew nuts and samosa. Daddy, please, can I have samosa on the train? Please... Please...last time mummy did not allow me, saying they made it in bad oil, but I saw the uncle making samosa and giving it to his son. He won't give his kid samosa cooked in bad oil, right daddy? Because he is the kid's father? Because mummy told me parents will never do things to hurt their babies. Right, daddy?"*

*"Ha! Ha! yes, sweetheart, we will never hurt you or do things that will hurt you, but you still cannot have anything from outside. I have packed plain cake, fresh bread, cashew nuts, cream biscuits, Frooti too, and mummy has made such yummy food for you guys, that I am jealous I will not be getting any of it myself,"* he said.

*"FROOTI! YAY! Thank you, daddy!!,"* said Pushki. Frooti was Pushki's favorite drink, it was mango juice sold in a small green carton with a red and white striped straw. It was her maternal grandfather, *Tatagaru*, who had bought her first Frooti when she was five years old. Since then, it was her most favorite thing on the planet.

Her *tatagaru* would buy her a small carton of Frooti and a small packet of cashew nuts every evening during her vacation, and they would both go for a long walk. It was their ritual every day, and as they walked, *tatagaru* would tell her many stories from the *Ramayana, Mahabharata, Krishna's stories, Panchatantra* and about two boys called *Tom Sawyer* and *Huckleberry Finn* and their adventures and about a man called *Gulliver* who landed on an island full of little men called *Lilliput*. Pushki was most excited about these stories of adventure that *tatagaru* narrated animatedly, as he acted out each part and modulated his voice as he spoke the dialogues of different characters. Pushki was looking forward to more such stories from her *tatagaru*.

The other fun part of Pushki's vacation was all the yummy food made by *ammamma*. *Ammamma* made Pushki's favorite items, like *Poha*, home-made potato chips, *Poori* and *aloo*. Ammamma was the best cook on the planet. Everyone said so! Pushki knew they were right. Ammamma would watch *Sanjeev Kapoor's Khana Khazana* cookery show religiously on TV, make notes and try new recipes. Pushki was always ready to try anything *ammamma* made, old or new. The thought of all the food made Pushki's mouth water.

It was almost a year since her last vacation with *ammamma* and *tatagaru* and Pushki could not wait for the journey to begin.

# Chapter 2

# The Journey Begins!

The next day, Daddy first loaded all their suitcases onto the overhead carrier of their car and tied everything with a thick rope to make sure that the luggage was secure. Next, all the smaller bags like the jute bag that had all the eatables, baby bag with cloth diapers and other baby supplies were kept in the boot of the car. Pushki bid farewell to her paternal grandparents and great-grandmother and then got into their car which was called the *Fiat Standard* (or as they simply called it, *"Standard"*). Daddy drove the *Standard* and in half an hour, they arrived at the Madras central station.

The Madras central station was a beautiful, big, red colored building. Mummy told Pushki that the British had built it. Pushki did not know who the British were. But she assumed that they must be people who liked making big, red colored buildings. *"Pushki, come to the side,"* said mummy as she got off the car slowly, holding Rinki in her arms. Daddy started unloading their luggage from the car as few porters (*Coolie*, daddy called them) approached them. Daddy spent some time arguing about the fare with them and finally selected a porter to carry their luggage. Daddy carried a *VIP* suitcase himself and mummy asked if Pushki could carry the *Kool Keg*, a small, round water container that everyone carried on such journeys. The porter walked in front of Pushki's family, carrying their suitcases stacked on top of each other, on his head. When they entered the central station, Pushki saw hundreds of people walking in all directions, most carrying luggage and many running behind their fast porters. There were more than ten platforms, Pushki wasn't sure how many, but could see one next to the other, some of them with trains on the track and some of them empty, waiting for a train to arrive. Daddy led everyone to a board and called Pushki to see it.

Daddy told Pushki that this was the information board, on which a list of trains was displayed. Daddy then pointed to 'Tamil Nadu Express' and told Pushki that it was the name of their train. He further explained, *"Every train has a number, Pushki, and every train has many compartments which are also numbered and every seat inside each compartment also has a number."*

*"So, what if someone else sits at my seat number?,"* asked Pushki. *"Then, you show them your ticket that has your seat number printed on it and tell them that they have made a mistake,"* replied daddy.

*"Okay, and what if the number on the ticket is not on the seat?,"* asked Pushki further.

*"Then, you have made a mistake darling,"* replied daddy.

*"Oh, but I don't want to make a mistake, daddy, I want to sit on the correct seat,"* said Pushki looking tense.

Daddy smiled and said, *"Well, that's why I am here, plus mummy is also going to be with you. We will make sure you are on the correct seat, ok?"*

Pushki agreed reluctantly, still unsure if her parents will find the right seat. *"What if they get the numbers mixed up or what if the train people forgot to put my seat number in the train?,"* she thought to herself. But she did not say anything to daddy and continued to walk with her family, carrying the *Kool Keg*.

Mummy had boiled water, filtered it using a white cloth and transferred it to the *Kool Keg* before they started to the central station. Mummy told Pushki that boiled water did not have germs, and so it was best they drank boiled water from the *Kool Keg* until the end of their journey. When mummy and Pushki went shopping, Pushki insisted on a red *Kool Keg* as she loved red. She loved wearing red dresses and had short hair. Short hair was not Pushki's choice, it was Mummy's. But, Pushki did not mind it since she could comb it quickly and rush out to play or sleep longer and still get ready for school quickly.

Inside the Central station, Pushki and her family walked with their *Coolie*, to their train, crossing many shops on the way. The smell of *vadas* being fried in hot oil wafted through the air, as they crossed a shop selling *Idly, Dosa, Vada, Pongal* and many other South Indian snacks and food items. They crossed shops selling filter coffee and chai, travel bags and accessories, clothes and much more. Pushki then saw a big, bright sign at a book shop. She stopped and slowly read the sign:

*"Hi-ggin-bo-thams,"* she said. She saw they had several books, comics, magazines and even newspapers there. Fascinated, she kept staring at the shop, when she heard daddy call out to her. Quickly, she ran to her parents and pointing at the shop said, *"Daddy, that shop is so nice! It is called Hi-ggin-something!"*

*"Yes, Pushki! Do you know that the Higginbotham's is the oldest bookstore in India? It was built way before India got its independence and guess what, there is a bigger store in Mount road too,* said daddy.

*"Wow daddy! Can we go there someday daddy? They must have so many books in the big store. I want to buy lots of books and start my own library daddy!* said Pushki excitedly.

*"Of course, dear, but don't you want to get to your train and go to ammamma's home? Come on now, it's getting late. We must get to the train and find your seats, or you will miss the train, Pushki!,"* said daddy trying to distract Pushki away from the bookstore.

*"Ok, daddy! But when I am back to Madras, you should take me to the Higgin book store. Okay, daddy? Please say yes,"* replied Pushki.

To this, Mummy chipped in saying, *"Yes dear, daddy will take you there when we are back, and it is called Higginbotham's. Pronounce it like this: Higg-in-bo-thams"*

*"Higg-in-bo-thams,"* repeated Pushki slowly.

*"Good girl. Now let's go before the Coolie disappears with our suitcases,"* joked daddy.

Soon, the family found their train and compartment (marked S5). Mummy and Daddy found their seats and the *Coolie* unloaded their luggage at their seats, help them arrange it under the lower berth and left with his pay. Pushki too double-checked that the numbers on their ticket matched the ones on their seats and she was very relieved! Now, no one is going to ask for her window seat!

Daddy went to the *Aavin* milk stall on the platform and got ice-cream for everyone. As they ate the ice-cream, daddy told Pushki to listen to mummy and stay safe, wished them all a happy journey and got off the train. He stood on the platform and waved goodbye to his girls. As the serpentine train slowly pulled out of the Madras central station around 2 p.m., Pushki waved eagerly and shouted through the window, *"Bye Daddy! See you after the holidays! I will miss you! BYE!"* and then climbed up to the top berth and promptly fell asleep. Carrying the *Kool Keg* along the long platform made her very tired!

Around 5 p.m., when Pushki woke up, she saw some more people in the adjoining seats. She climbed down the berth and mummy introduced her to a nice lady called Saroja aunty. Rinki was asleep and so Pushki asked mummy if they could play the *snakes and ladder* game. Mummy agreed and soon they were happily playing the game. After some time Saroja aunty wanted to play too, so they all played *Ludo* together. Pushki did not understand the rules of *Ludo* but she liked rolling the dice, so played it happily.

Soon, Rinki woke up and mummy was busy feeding her. Rinki usually drank milk and sometimes ate baby formula mixed in warm water. Pushki did not want to disturb mummy and so sat at her favorite window seat quietly and looked at the fast-disappearing trees, bushes, fields, houses and clouds. The rhythmic chugging of the train made Pushki yawn. Soon, it was night time and after having *lemon rice* and fried potatoes for dinner, Pushki went to sleep peacefully.

Early next morning around 5 a.m., Pushki woke up as she heard her baby sister Rinki wailing. Mummy was mixing baby formula but Rinki was very hungry and did not know how to talk yet, so she cried whenever she wanted to say something. Pushki tried telling Rinki that mummy was mixing food for her and it will take few minutes to get the food ready, but Rinki gave her a confused smile and went back to crying. Somehow mummy managed to mix the baby formula quickly and gave it to Rinki, who promptly slept off as soon as she finished eating. But mummy looked very worried. Hearing Rinki's crying, few other aunties in the adjoining berths woke up too and were talking to mummy.

Pushki heard mummy telling Saroja aunty that she somehow forgot to bring Rinki's milk bottles and was not sure what to do when Rinki woke up again in 2–3 hours, as Rinki liked milk more than baby formula. The train had already crossed Vijayawada station and mummy had asked in the train pantry if they had any milk and they said no. Then, Saroja aunty told mummy that the train would reach its next station, Warangal, at around 7 a.m. and would stop there for 15 minutes. So, mummy would have enough time to get off the train and buy boiled milk for Rinki from a tea shop at the station and come back in time before the train started again.

Mummy asked Pushki if she will be ok if mummy went to buy milk for Rinki and Pushki said yes. Pushki knew that Nagpur was their destination and that mummy would be back fast. Mummy usually did many things super-fast. So, Pushki was not worried. Mummy made Pushki brush, gave her a wet-towel bath, changed her dress and gave her some bread and jam to eat. Rinki was still asleep so Pushki and mummy were waiting for Warangal to come.

*"I will be back in ten minutes, maximum, Pushki. You must not go anywhere, ok?,"* asked mummy anxiously. Mummy knew that if she took Pushki along, they would be slow, and they might miss the train and be stranded at Warangal. The luggage was also heavy to carry; hence it was best Pushki stayed in the train. When the train stopped at Warangal, mummy got down onto the platform and dashed with Rinki to buy the milk and come back as fast as possible.

# Chapter 3

# Warangal

Around 7 a.m., the *Tamil Nadu express* pulled into Warangal station and mummy got off the train with Rinki and 10 rupees in hand. Since it was winter time, it was very foggy that morning and Pushki soon saw mummy disappear into the fog. Pushki kept looking out of the window trying to look for mummy and in between, kept checking on their luggage too.

*"Don't worry, child, your mother will be back soon,"* said Saroja aunty. But, Pushki was not worried. Maybe a little worried because she was not sure which way mummy went. She kept checking the new watch daddy gave her as a vacation present. It was a toy watch, but it showed the time, unlike the toy watches some of her friends had. Soon, five minutes passed and then ten and then fifteen and there was still no sign of mummy. Even Saroja aunty got up and peered out of the window, trying to get a clear look outside. She murmured something and went to talk to few other passengers. Few uncles went to the doors of the compartment to check if mummy had walked past them and went into some other compartment. Suddenly, the train horn went off and the train started moving! Without mummy!

Mummy got off the train and frantically rushed towards the shops in the station, looking for a tea shop. Luckily, she found one and quickly bought milk to last the day. Rinki was still asleep on her left shoulder. Mummy got the milk bottle and change back, thanked the tea shop person and quickly made her way back to the train. Since it was very foggy, she could not see the train clearly and was unsure where her compartment was. Suddenly, she noticed a strange man following her, and she walked faster, parallel to the train, and went so far ahead that she found herself at the engine. Exactly at that point the train horn went off! Mummy panicked, ran back and got into the first compartment's door that was right behind the train's engine and then the train started.

Mummy thought that the train would be interconnected through the vestibule and she could walk inside the train to her compartment, which was the 4th or 5th compartment behind the engine as far as she could remember. But as soon as she got into the compartment, she saw it was full of men from the Indian Army who were equally puzzled to see a woman with a baby suddenly jump into their compartment. The Army men then told mummy that the first three compartments were booked for them and that they were not connected to the 4th compartment. When she realized what had happened, mummy started sobbing. The train horn had disturbed Rinki's sleep who promptly started crying the roof down. The baffled army men had no idea who this mother and child were and why they were both crying at the same time!

# Chapter 4

# The (Mis) Adventure!

One of the army men, Major Singh, told mummy to calm down and that everything would be alright. He said that they were all men of the Indian army and would do everything to help her. The other army men nodded, agreeing with Major Singh, and offered a seat for mummy to sit. Mummy thanked them and first fed Rinki some milk which she got from Warangal station to calm her down and put her to sleep. Next, mummy explained to the army men what had happened. After listening to her ordeal, Major Singh told mummy not to worry and that the train would reach Balharshah Junction around 11 a.m. and they would all help mummy and Rinki re-unite with Pushki. Mummy thanked them again, but they said it was their duty to help every Indian, so thanks was not necessary! Mummy gave a small smile but was worried internally, since Pushki would be alone for almost 4 hours and mummy thought to herself: what if Pushki had gotten off the train at Warangal looking for her? She knew Pushki was a smart kid but was not sure how she was doing now.

After the train left without mummy, everyone in the compartment was tense. Pushki heard people saying that maybe mummy left because she did not want two girl children or that she may be stranded back in Warangal station. Pushki knew that her Mummy and Daddy loved her and Rinki. In fact, when Rinki was born, some people told daddy, *"Better luck next time!,"* but daddy bought chocolates that day to celebrate Rinki's arrival and made Pushki distribute it to everyone at the hospital.

Daddy told Pushki, *"Rinki will be your best friend when you grow up and you both can do whatever you want, never think you are any less, Princess."* Plus, given how silly the boys in her class were, Pushki was sure her mummy was happy she had two daughters.

As the train sped along, Pushki sat quietly, looking out of the train window, gazing at the vast green fields and the blue sky lined with plenty of white cotton-like clouds. *"Where did mummy go?,"* she thought to herself. *"She surely has not left me and gone; maybe she got stuck somewhere?,"* her mind tried to find reason. She sighed and drank some water. The sun was shining bright today, making her thirsty. *"Is Rinki also thirsty? Maybe she is…but Rinki is a small baby, she cannot even say she is thirsty…,"* thoughts were moving along rapidly in Pushki's mind, when suddenly one scary thought hit her, *"What if Rinki is not with mummy? Did mummy leave Rinki and go away too? But mummy would never do that… Where did mummy and Rinki go?,"* she continued to wonder.

*"I think this is what baby cloud felt like too,"* Pushki suddenly remembered the story of the baby cloud which daddy had told her. Whenever she would ask daddy for a story, he would tell her the story of the baby cloud. Even when she asked him for a new story, daddy would say that he knew only one story. But it was Pushki's favorite story and she loved it every time daddy narrated it to her.

Pushki smiled to herself and recollected the baby cloud story: *There was once a family of clouds, Papa cloud, Mamma cloud and Baby cloud, who would travel around the world and do their shake-dance to make it rain.* Daddy said shake-dance was like the break dance of the clouds. Pushki did not know what break dance was but was happy that in shake-dance the clouds did not break anything.

*Every time the cloud family finished their shake-dance, they would take rest and wait for the wind to take them to their next place of visit. Once, baby cloud was very tired as he shake-danced a lot, trying to make it rain as much as mamma and papa cloud did. He wanted them to be proud of him. Mamma cloud told him, he would be able to make it rain more as he grew up, but baby cloud tried to make it rain a lot anyway. This made him tired and he really wanted to sleep. Papa cloud told him to stay awake for some more time as the wind was very powerful and he won't be able to hold baby cloud if he slept off. Baby cloud did not listen to papa cloud and slept off. Soon, the wind came and took mamma and papa cloud away, who kept calling out to baby cloud, but he was fast asleep and did not hear them shout his name.*

*When he woke up, it was nice and bright as the sun was back. Baby cloud realized that he was the only one left! He cried for days because he missed his mamma and papa and when he cried, people under him on planet earth were annoyed with him, as he was not enough to make it rain or give them shade. He figured even they missed his family and the entire cloud community. Soon, days turned into seasons and after four seasons passed, one day he saw mamma and papa cloud rush to him. Baby cloud was thrilled to see them, and they all gave each other their family group hug and did shake-dance together and made it rain nicely. It was the happiest day of baby cloud's life and he saw people on earth also dance in the rain they created.*

*"The earth is round, baby, said papa cloud, so we went around it and came back for you! Wind helped us too, he said sorry as he somehow missed taking you along last time but this time, we will make sure we all go together but you must promise not to sleep off again!" Baby cloud agreed immediately!"*

Recollecting the baby cloud story, Pushki cheered up quickly. *"Even if mummy did go away or get left behind, she can walk around the world and find me again!,"* she thought to herself. She told herself determined, *"I will have to wait for four seasons at the maximum, and then I can meet mummy and Rinki again!"*

Pushki suddenly remembered something and excitedly, she turned to Saroja aunty and said, *"Don't worry aunty, I know that after Tamil Nadu express, the next train is Grand Trunk (GT) express. Mummy will get into GT and come. There will be maximum few hours delay but I can manage because my tatagaru, my mother's father, will be waiting for us at Nagpur station. If you just help me carry the luggage down from the train on to the platform, I can manage!"*

Everyone was shocked for a second at Pushki's statement and then burst out laughing. Pushki said indignantly, *"I am a small kid! How can I carry such heavy suitcases and bags? My tatagaru is also an old man and a heart-patient! Come on, you should help me. Just carry them to the platform for me and then we will get a coolie from there!"*

Saroja aunty gave a big smile and said to the others, *"See how brave this young one is! The mother is gone for over an hour now and this child is not even crying!"*

Pushki: *"But, aunty, my mummy will come back. I am sure she is in Warangal or maybe she got into the wrong compartment with the wrong seat number and is searching for the right seat number. It took us a while to find our seats too, before the train started in Madras. Also, see I have the ticket with me!"* Pushki opened the big brown ticket and showed it to everyone looking at her. *"So, I am sure mummy forgot our seat numbers and is searching for us in this long train!"*

# Chapter 5

# The Red Signal

An hour after the train left Warangal, Rinki woke up and looked confused staring at all the army men. But she saw mummy's face and smiled. Soon, some of the army men started singing movie songs and Rinki started laughing and enjoying their performance. An orderly, called Samarth, offered a banana to Rinki. Mummy accepted it, broke a small piece from the banana, made it into a paste by crushing it with her fingers and then gave it to Rinki to eat. Rinki gave a puzzled look but she liked the taste of the banana and continued to eat without a fuss.

Two hours had passed by since the train left Warangal station, when it stopped again due to a red signal. Although it was in the wilderness and there was no platform to get down on to, Major Singh suggested to mummy that they could get off the train and quickly walk back to her compartment and that he would help carry the baby and walk ahead of her. Mummy agreed because she was worried about Pushki and wanted to come back to her as fast as possible.

They entire contingent said goodbye to mummy and Rinki quickly. Although they were sad to see Rinki go, they were happy that mummy and Rinki would meet Pushki. Some of them walked with mummy and Major Singh to the end of the third compartment and helped mummy climb down the three steps of the compartment's door onto the gravel, and Major Singh got down carefully holding Rinki. Major Singh quickly dashed across the compartments and reached the fifth compartment where Pushki was.

He quickly got in and shouted *"Pushki! Are you here? Rinki's sister Pushki!"* Pushki was so thrilled to see Rinki, who saw Pushki's face and gave the widest toothless smile! Pushki rushed to the officer and took Rinki from him and said, *"Thank you, uncle! But where is mummy?!"* Major Singh turned and looked behind him puzzled, and mummy was nowhere to be seen! And the train started moving again!!

Mummy was close behind Major Singh, trying to be as quick as she could, but the gravel stones and her saree were making it tough to run. Soon, the distance between her and Major Singh increased and suddenly the train horn went off! She cried out in despair as she saw the army officer get into the 5th compartment with Rinki and she was only near the fourth!

People in the 4th compartment saw a man in army uniform running with a baby followed by a woman who screamed when the train horn went off. Not knowing what was happening, some people pulled mummy into the 4th compartment as the train started to move. Mummy got in and ran to the vestibule only to find it disconnected too! Mummy collapsed on the floor sobbing, first she had lost one daughter and now she lost both!

# Chapter 6

# The Wait for Balharshah Junction

The army officer explained to Saroja aunty and the others what had happened, and everyone was thankful that the baby (Rinki) was safe, but they were all now tense about mummy. Did she get into the 4th compartment? Or is she now stranded in the wilderness? Should someone pull the chain and stop the train? The debate was raging on.

Meanwhile, Pushki was thrilled to see Rinki. She held her and smiled at her, Rinki also smiled back, happy to see a familiar face after such a long time. After some time, Rinki was hungry again but the milk bottle was either with mummy or lost in all the confusion. *"The next station, Balharshah Junction, is still around two hours away,"* said Saroja aunty to Pushki. People tried to offer food to Pushki but Pushki said, *"Thank you, but I cannot accept food from strangers! Mummy's strict rule!"*

Rinki was now crying a lot, so Pushki tried to think what she had that she could give Rinki to eat. Rinki did not have teeth yet so she needed something that was soft, thought Pushki. She quickly went through the bag daddy gave her and found plain cake and biscuits in it. The cake was as soft as sponge, so Pushki asked Saroja aunty to hold Rinki in her lap and squished the cake with her little fingers and gave it to Rinki to eat. Rinki made a face at the beginning but slowly kept eating little pieces. Pushki took a water bottle's cap and put very small pieces of cake in it and added 3–4 drops of water from the *Kool Keg* and pressed it well to make it into a soft paste. Now, Rinki was able to eat it happily and she ate well and stopped crying too.

After mummy finished crying and was exhausted, people in the 4th compartment told her that since it was the unreserved section, it was also not connected to rest of the train that had compartments of the reserved section. Mummy then explained to them about all the misadventure since morning and she had a shocked audience, that mostly chided her for travelling alone with two small children, but some of them gave her support and said Balharshah Junction was 90 minutes away and she would be with her daughters soon. Mummy prayed silently that both her children must be safe and not hungry, and she also vowed she would never leave either of them alone ever again!

Those 90 minutes of wait were the longest for mummy and Pushki. *"Come back soon, mummy,"* Pushki whispered softly, as she looked out of the window, with Rinki now asleep in her lap. *"Maybe she is dreaming of cake,"* thought Pushki when she saw Rinki smile in her sleep.

# Chapter 7

# The Reunion

Finally, when the *Tamil Nadu express* entered Balharshah Junction, mummy ran out of the 4th compartment to the platform and then into the 5th compartment and Pushki was also looking eagerly at either door of the compartment. Mummy ran in and hugged Pushki and said, *"I am so sorry sweetheart! I should have never left you here alone, I am so very sorry!"* Pushki was just happy to see mummy again and Rinki woke up and gave her trademark toothless smile. All was well again and Pushki heard some uncle telling mummy that if she wanted any more milk for the baby, he would go and get it! Everyone burst out laughing and started clapping!

It was soon lunch time and literally everyone in the compartment came to see mummy, Pushki and Rinki reunited. The story had spread to rest of the train, so they had some visitors from other compartments too! Saroja aunty offered some lunch to mummy, who gladly accepted it. Mummy said, *"I am so thankful Saroja ji, you took good care of my Pushki."*

Saroja aunty: *"Ha! Ha! Good joke! Your son needed no taking care of! He was so brave! He did not even take the food I offered him, saying you told him not to accept food from strangers Ha! Ha! Ha!"*

Mummy (looking embarrassed): *"Well, you see, these days it is hard to trust people, but I am sure she did not mean any offense. Wait, what?! She is my daughter! Not my son! She is a girl!"*

Saroja aunty (looking genuinely surprised): *"Is it?! Oh my god! We all thought it was a little boy because she was wearing a shirt, and pant and had short hair! Plus, he was so brave and calm throughout! Oh sorry, I mean she!"*

Pushki (annoyed), *"Aunty, wait a minute! I am a girl and I am also brave! Do you want me to prove to you that I am a girl?!*

Mummy (worried): *"Pushki, what are you saying?"*

Pushki: *"Wait, I will prove it to everyone right here, right now, that I am a girl!"*

Mummy (panicking): *"Pushki, there is no need…"*

Pushki pulled out her bag from under the lower berth and opened it and removed one dress after another, opening them and showing to Saroja aunty and everyone else gathered;

*"See! I told you I am a girl! Why will I have frocks, skirts and dresses in my bag if I was a boy? Are you happy now with the proof that I am a girl?"*

Everyone laughed uncontrollably and Saroja aunty said to Pushki, *"Ok dear, I accept defeat. You are a girl and a brave one too!"*

Saroja aunty then gave Pushki a big hug and through rest of the journey, everyone was praising the brave little girl who did not panic or cry when her mother was gone and even took care of her baby sister well.

# Epilogue

Nagpur arrived soon and Pushki met her beloved *tatagaru* and immediately told him everything about her first train adventure. *Tatagaru* was shocked initially but said he was happy that all his girls were safe. They then took the bus from Nagpur to Balaghat and then another bus from Balaghat to Malanjhkhand.

When they reached home, Pushki finally met her *ammamma* and told her the entire story too. *Ammamma* told her, *"Of course girls are brave! There is no difference, Pushki. Outward, we may all look different from each other but inside, we are all the same."*

As Pushki listened attentively, *ammamma* continued, *"We may feel scared sometimes but each one of us has it in us to get over our fears and face situations bravely. I am so proud of you, Pushki. In the time of hardship, you stayed calm and even took good care of Rinki. This is your first adventure and I am sure a brave girl like you will have many more such wonderful, sometimes scary, adventures but you will surely live to tell the tale. Now, go have a bath and come to eat because I have made your favorite Poha and potato chips!"*

*"POHA!,"* screamed Pushki gleefully and ran to have a bath. After an exciting train adventure, she was finally at her *ammamma's* home and could not wait for her vacation to begin!

Scan to digitally connect with the official website.

Visit www.qrsecurelog.in for more details.

~PSIA information can be obtained
www.ICGtesting.com
~ed in the USA
V021938080623
~BV00013B/653